This book belongs to
my friend:

_____

A NOTE TO PARENTS

Schoolmates, the community playground, and even siblings can bring out the competitive spirit in your child. A little healthy competition is a good thing. But as Little Bill discovers in *Sports Day*, playing with and being supportive of friends is just as important as winning.

As you read the story, emphasize that Little Bill and his friends are all planning and contributing to the event in their own special way. Discuss Little Bill's actions throughout the story. Is he having fun? Is it because he is winning or is it due to other reasons? Point out Little Bill's good sportsmanship and selfless attitude.

Plan a backyard version of *Sports Day* for your child and her friends. Ask every child to offer an idea for a game or bring an item to share. Include some of the games Little Bill and his friends play as well as your child's favorites. You might want to encourage your child to make some sort of souvenir for all participants. Encourage everyone to do their best while focusing on the enjoyment of simply being together.

Learning Fundamental: **emotions**

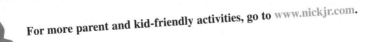
For more parent and kid-friendly activities, go to www.nickjr.com.

Sports Day

Published by Scholastic Inc., 90 Old Sherman Turnpike, Danbury, CT 06816

SCHOLASTIC and associated logos are trademarks and/or registered trademarks of Scholastic Inc.

ISBN 0-7172-6630-3

Printed in the U.S.A.

First Scholastic Printing, February 2003

Sports Day

by
LaVonne Carlson

illustrated by
Dan Kanemoto

SCHOLASTIC INC.

New York Toronto London Auckland Sydney
Mexico City New Delhi Hong Kong Buenos Aires

"Ready or not, here I come!" called Little Bill. He uncovered his eyes and began searching for his friends' hiding places.

Just then his sister, April, and brother, Bobby, ran up to him from across the park.

"Look what I just won!" shouted April.

Little Bill and his friends crowded around April to see what she was holding.

"Wow! Look at that medal!" said Little Bill. "How did you get it?"

"I won the basketball free-throw contest at my school's Sports Day," April explained.

"That's great!" exclaimed Little Bill.

"I wish we could have a basketball contest," added Monty.

"I have an idea," said Little Bill. "Let's have our own Sports Day!"

"That's a great idea!" Dorado clapped.

"We can have lots of different games, and we can all play," said Fuchsia.

"Let's all meet here tomorrow," said Andrew.

"Hooray!" everyone cheered.

"You know, planning a Sports Day takes a lot of work," Bobby said.

"Can you help us get ready?" asked Little Bill.

"Sure," Bobby agreed. He told everyone what to bring to make the Sports Day a success.

Fuchsia and Kiku agreed to bring the sports equipment.

Monty volunteered to make the sign.
Dorado said he'd bring water.

Andrew decided to bring snacks.

"I can help, too," said April. "I'll be the referee, so I'll bring my whistle."

"And I'll keep score, so I'll bring scorecards," added Bobby. "I think that's everything we need."

"Little Bill, what are going to bring?" asked Andrew.
"I don't know yet, but I'll think of something,"
answered Little Bill.

At dinner that night, Little Bill told his parents about Sports Day. "I hope I win something like April did," he said.

"Winning is nice, Little Bill," said his father. "But the best part about Sports Day will be playing with your friends."

"That's right," added Little Bill's mother. "When everyone has a good time, everyone wins."

After dinner, Little Bill thought about what he could bring to Sports Day. Suddenly he had an idea. He ran to find Alice the Great, his great-grandmother.

"I want to make a surprise for Sports Day," he told her. "Will you help me?"

"Of course, Little Bill," Alice the Great assured him. "What is your idea?"

Little Bill whispered his idea in her ear.

"That will be a wonderful surprise," she said.

The next day, Little Bill and his friends met at the
park. They were jumping with excitement.

April blew her whistle. "Hey, everybody!" she
exclaimed. "Are you ready to get Sports Day started?"
"Yup. I'm ready to play!" hollered Little Bill.
"Me, too!" everyone else chimed in.

The first event was the three-legged race. "Ready, set, go!" April shouted.

Right away, Andrew and Little Bill's legs got twisted. They laughed so hard that they fell down. As they struggled to get up, Fuchsia and Kiku easily crossed the finish line first.

The basketball toss came next. Everyone's score was close until the end, when Monty made two shots from far away.

The next event was the sprint. They were all neck and neck, but at the last second, Andrew ran just a little bit faster than everyone else and won the race.

Soon it was time for the last event—the egg walk.
Little Bill was in the lead, trying hard to keep his egg
balanced. But just before the finish line, he hiccuped
and the egg fell. Dorado crossed the finish line first.

Little Bill laughed. "Con-*hiccup*-gratula-*hiccup*-tions!"
he said to Dorado.

April blew her whistle. "Good job, everyone," she called. "I think Sports Day was a big success!"

"I had such a good time!" said Monty.
"I can't believe it's over," sighed Kiku.

"Wait!" said Little Bill, jumping up. "It isn't over yet!"
He ran over to Alice the Great and returned with a box.
"I have a surprise," he told his friends.

Little Bill opened the box and exclaimed, "I made ribbons for all the winners!"

Little Bill's friends admired their bright blue ribbons. Then Fuchsia cried, "Oh, no, Little Bill! You don't have a ribbon."

"Oh, that's okay," he said. "I just had a great time playing with everybody."

"You're right, Little Bill," Monty said. "That was the best part."

"Wait!" Fuchsia said, looking inside the box. "Look! There's one blue ribbon left."

"That one's for you, Little Bill," said Kiku. "Now we all have a ribbon!"

Dorado picked up the ribbon and gave it to Little Bill.
"We all had a good time, so we all won," laughed
Little Bill.

After everyone finished cleaning up and saying good-bye, Little Bill and Andrew walked home.

"I'd like to have another Sports Day tomorrow," Andrew said.

"That's a great idea!" said Little Bill. "We can call it the Winning-est Sports Day!"

"Yeah!" Andrew agreed.

"But why wait until tomorrow?" asked Little Bill. "I'll race you to the steps right now!"